Plip and Plop

First published in 2002 by
Franklin Watts
96 Leonard Street
London
EC2A 4XD

Franklin Watts Australia
45–51 Huntley Street
Alexandria
NSW 2015

A CIP catalogue record for this book is available
from the British Library.

ISBN 0 7496 4474 5 (hbk)
ISBN 0 7496 4620 9 (pbk)

Series Editor: Louise John
Series Advisor: Dr Barrie Wade
Cover Design: Jason Anscomb
Design: Peter Scoulding

Printed in China

HOPSCOTCH

Plip and Plop

by Penny Dolan and Lisa Smith

W
FRANKLIN WATTS
LONDON•SYDNEY

Next to Grandpa's house stood a
big beech tree. Sam liked that tree.

At the end of Grandpa's garden
lived two pigeons, Plip and Plop.
They liked the big beech tree, too,
and one morning they moved in.

Plip and Plop flew over
Grandpa's grass.
They perched above
the porch.

They strutted along the fence.

They swung on the washing line.

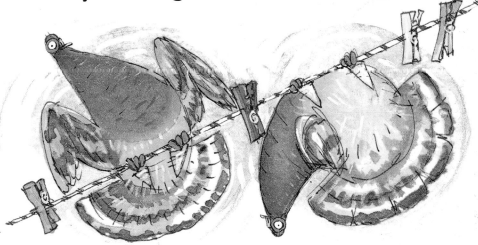

And if anyone went into the
garden, Plip and Plop got busy...

Plip! A blob landed on
Grandpa's shoulder.
Plop! More on Gran's hair.

Plip! Another blob on Sam's hand – just as he was eating his ice cream. "Ugh!" he shouted.

Plip plop, plip plop, everywhere –
on the washing, on the chairs,
everywhere! It was terrible.

"They make such a mess,"
sighed Gran.

Usually it was fun staying with Gran and Grandpa. This time Sam couldn't play football, climb the tree or do anything outside.

Plip and Plop fluttered around all
the time, and everywhere they
went, they plipped and plopped.

"I wish those birds would go away," sighed Gran.

Grandpa took Sam to the garden centre. While Grandpa looked around, Sam was busy thinking about Plip and Plop.

"Grandpa," he said.

"I've got an idea."

Grandpa and Sam arrived home,
carrying a big package.

"Whatever are you two doing?"
called Gran.

"Wait and see!" giggled Sam.

Grandpa and Sam waited.
Down flew Plip and Plop,
ready for action.

Grandpa gently turned on
the new hose.

Splash! A spray of silvery water
landed on Plip.

Splosh! Another one landed on Plop.

"Got you!" shouted Sam.

The pesky pair flew back to the big beech tree. They perched on a branch, shaking their wet feathers and looking very surprised.

Then down they flew again. This time it was Grandpa's turn with the long green hose.

Everywhere those birds landed, they got soaked.

Soon Plip and Plop felt too wet to plip and plop. They didn't like being near the tree any more.

They flew off towards the very end
of the garden.

"You two must be wet through!"
laughed Gran, bringing out towels.
But Sam didn't care!

The sun was shining, and everyone could have fun in the garden again – without those pesky pigeons!

As for Plip and Plop, they stayed happily at the other end of the garden. It was much better than living in the big beech tree!

Hopscotch has been specially designed to fit the requirements of the National Literacy Strategy. It offers real books by top authors and illustrators for children developing their reading skills.

There are five other Hopscotch stories to choose from:

Marvin, the Blue Pig
Written by Karen Wallace, illustrated by Lisa Williams
Marvin is the only blue pig on the farm. He tries hard to make himself pink but nothing seems to work. Then, one day, his friend Esther gives him some advice...

The Queen's Dragon
Written by Anne Cassidy, illustrated by Gwyneth Williamson
The Queen is fed up with her dragon, Harry. His wings are floppy and his fire has gone out! She decides to find a new one, but it's not quite as easy as she thinks...

Flora McQuack
Written by Penny Dolan, illustrated by Kay Widdowson
Flora McQuack finds a lost egg by the side of the loch and decides to hatch it. But when the egg cracks open, Flora is in for a surprise!

Naughty Nancy
Written by Anne Cassidy, illustrated by Desideria Guicciardini
Norman's little sister Nancy is the naughtiest girl he knows. When Mum goes out for the day, Norman tries hard to keep Nancy out of trouble, but things don't quite go according to plan!

Willie the Whale
Written by Joy Oades, illustrated by Barbara Vagnozzi
Willie the Whale decides to go on a round-the-world adventure – from the South Pole to the desert and even to New York. But is the city really the place for a big, friendly whale?